Curious George™

MY FIRST
BEDTIME STORIES

Houghton Mifflin Harcourt

Boston   New York

Contents

Curious George: Are You Curious?

This is George.
George is a good little monkey
and always very curious.

Do you ever feel like George?

Do you ever feel happy?

Are you
sometimes loud?

Have you ever felt scared...

or hurt...

or proud?

Do you ever feel sick…

or dizzy?

Are you sometimes sad . . .

or silly?

Have you ever felt so naughty...

that you needed a time-out?

Are you mischievous?

Are you curious?

Do you ever feel like George?

Curious George and the Firefighters

This is George.
He was a good little monkey and always very curious. Today George and the man with the yellow hat were on a field trip to the fire station.

The fire chief was waiting for them right next to the big red fire truck. "Welcome!" he said, and he led everyone upstairs to begin their tour.

George was curious about everything in the fire station. He slid down the pole. There was a great big fire truck and a whole wall full of coats, hats, and big black boots!

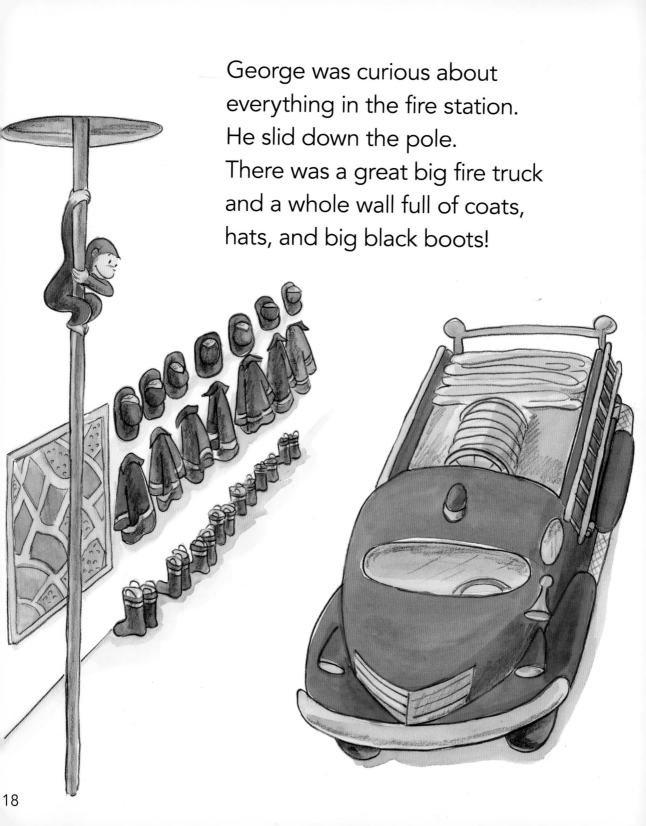

George tried on a pair
of boots.

Next, he picked out a helmet.

And, finally, George put on
a jacket. He was a firefighter!

Suddenly . . . *BRRRIINNGG!*

The firefighters rushed in and jumped into the fire truck.

And so did George.

The truck went fast to get to the fire.
"*WHOO WHOO WHOO*," went the
whistle and George held on tight.

Whoo Whoo Whoooo

The fire was at a pizza parlor on Main Street.
Smoke was coming out of a window in the
back and a crowd was gathering in the street.

The firefighters rushed off the truck
and started unwinding their hose.
They knew just what to do.
And George was ready to help.
Together they put out the fire as
quick as can be! Hurray!

Before long the fire truck was back at the fire
station, where a familiar voice called, "George!"
It was the man with the yellow hat.
"This little monkey had quite an adventure,"
said one of the firefighters.

For a final treat, all the children got to take a ride around the neighborhood on the shiny red fire truck. What a brave little monkey!

Curious George's Day at the Farm

Today George and the man with the yellow hat are visiting the Jackson Family Farm.

There is so much to explore and many animals to meet. George is going to have lots of fun!

Millie the cow is ready to be milked, and George is going to help. But Mr. Jackson needs his stool to sit on and his pail to catch the milk.

George will fill the bottles.
Can you find the things they need?

Next, George will gather eggs in the henhouse.
There are hens and chicks everywhere!
"Cheep, cheep!" the chicks say.

George is curious.
How many eggs will he find?
Can you count the eggs and the chicks, too?

Who's ready for a snack? George is!
But he helps Mr. Jackson feed the other
animals first: There's hay for the horse and cow,
milk for the lamb, slop for the pigs, and some
water for Sparky. And, of course, the perfect
treat for George: a banana cream pie!

When snack time is over George and Mr. Jackson harvest a rainbow of vegetables. Carrots, beans, lettuce, celery, potatoes, cauliflower, and more!

Which colors does George see?

George ends his day with a bouncy, bumpy hayride out to the pumpkin patch. He and Sparky pick out the biggest pumpkin they can find for George to take home.

What a wonderful day at the farm!

Curious George Goes to a Bookstore

Today George and his friend the man with the yellow hat were going to the grand opening of a bookstore in their neighborhood.

George looked around the bookstore. So many books! What stories would they hold inside? What funny characters would he meet?

George saw a giant display of science books.
It was hard to resist for a little monkey who
loves to climb!

From higher up George
saw a crowd gathered
around a table.
George was
curious.

The crowd was waiting to meet the author
of the Penny the Penguin books.

George wanted to meet her, too!
George joined the long line.

Finally it was George's turn!

The manager asked George if he would like to help with the signing. George was delighted.

George made sure each
book was opened to the
right page, ready for
the author's signature.

As she finished signing the last book, the author turned
to George and smiled. "Thank you so much for all of your
help today. Would you like me to sign your book, too?"

George did! He loved his new book. It was special and one of a kind. He'd had such a fun day at the bookstore and he couldn't wait to visit again.

Curious George Loves to Ride

This is George.
He is a good little monkey and always very curious.
George loves to go places and is always ready to
ride off on an adventure.

What do you think George
rides around his room?

He rides a ball!

What does George ride
at the circus?

A bicycle!

What will George ride
to get downtown?

A taxicab?

A subway train?

No. George likes to
ride the bus.

How does George ride high
up in the sky?

He hangs
from balloons,

and glides on a kite,

and sometimes he rides
in a helicopter!

But when George is ready
to go home . . .

he rides in the little blue car with his
friend the man with the yellow hat.

Goodbye, George!

Good Night, Curious George

George has had a long, fun day
of jumping, climbing, monkey play.

Now sun is setting, sleepyhead.
Pick up those toys. It's time for bed.

First, we fill the tub right up
with soap and water, rubber duck.

A bubbly bath cleans monkey toes,
belly, arms, back, and nose.

Cozy things help George sleep tight
all the way through the night.

Striped pajamas, soft to wear.
Comfy slippers, cuddly bear.

George sleeps best with a full tummy.
He wants something yellow and yummy.

A bedtime snack—not too sweet.
Two more bites, then brush those teeth.

Done with running, playing, and leaping,
now it's time to think about sleeping.

One more story, sing a song.
He's yawning now—it won't be long.

With cozy sheets and his soft teddy,
sleepy George is finally ready.

Under the covers,
turn out the light.

Sleep well, little monkey.
Sweet dreams, good night.

hmhbooks.com
curiousgeorge.com

ISBN: 978-0-358-16403-6

Manufactured in China
SCP 10 9 8 7 6 5 4 3 2 1
4500764575